MY NEW BEST FRIEND

To Beckett and Adalyn.
With gratitude for Serena,
who inspired this book.—S. M.

Wisdom Publications
199 Elm Street
Somerville, MA 02144 USA
wisdompubs.org

Library of Congress Cataloging-in-Publication Data

Names: Marlowe, Sara (Sara Gwynn), 1973– author. | Salom, Ivette, illustrator.
Title: My new best friend / by Sara Marlowe ; illustrated by Ivette Salom.
Description: Somerville, MA : Wisdom Publications, [2016] | Summary: A young
   girl reveals how she can be a best friend to herself, providing
   encouragement, patience, and acceptance. | Description based on print
   version record and CIP data provided by publisher; resource not viewed.
Identifiers: LCCN 2016020932 (print) | LCCN 2016000555 (ebook) | ISBN
   9781614293712 (ebook) | ISBN 1614293716 (ebook) | ISBN 9781614293538
   (hardcover : alk. paper)
Subjects: | CYAC: Best friends—Fiction. | Friendship—Fiction. |
   Self-acceptance—Fiction. | Awareness—Fiction.
Classification: LCC PZ7.M3455 (print) | LCC PZ7.M3455 My 2016 (ebook) | DDC
   [E]—dc23
LC record available at https://lccn.loc.gov/2016020932

ISBN 978-1-61429-353-8
Ebook ISBN 978-1-61429-371-2

20 19 18 17 16
5   4   3   2   1

Artwork by Ivette Salom. Cover and interior design by Annie Beth Ericsson.
Set in Mama Bear 21/29.

Printed in the PRC.

MY NEW BEST FRIEND

By **Sara Marlowe**

Illustrated by **Ivette Salom**

Wisdom

I have a new best friend.
I've known her my whole life,
but we only just became friends.

We have many
adventures.

She is always by my side,
when I'm having fun and
even when I'm not.

When I feel sad,

she comforts me.

When I feel frustrated,

she reminds me I'm doing my best.

When I feel worried,

she takes a deep breath with me.

When I feel happy,
she takes the time to notice.

She is gentle when
accidents happen.

You worked
so hard on
that.

She is patient when I'm having a hard day.

She encourages me
to follow my dreams.

My new best friend offers me kind words every day.

She wishes me to be happy, healthy, and peaceful.

She knows me best and
loves me just as I am.

I know she will always
be there for me.

Any guesses who my new best friend might be?

Let me introduce you...

My new best friend is **me**!

What is self-compassion?

When people we care about are having a hard time, we usually treat them with kindness and understanding. Yet when we are the ones having a hard time, we are often quick to be unkind. We may get angry and impatient with ourselves, even calling ourselves nasty names. We might call this inner bullying.

Instead, we can learn to treat ourselves with kindness and understanding, especially when we are having a hard time. We can notice and accept our feelings—just as our family, close friends, and even our pets accept us. We all feel sad, angry, and worried sometimes. When these feelings come, we can gently notice what is happening with kindness and an open heart. When we feel happy, we can take time to notice that. When something goes well for us, we can pause and appreciate our accomplishment, large or small.

Keep yourself in good company. You're always by your side, so go ahead—be your own best friend!